Groovy Girls™
Sleep Over Club

The First Pajama Party
Slumberrific Six

Robin Epstein

Scholastic Inc.

New York Toronto London Auckland Sydney
Mexico City New Delhi Hong Kong Buenos Aires

Read all the books about the Groovy Girls!

For Mom and Dad,
always

Cover illustration by Taia Morley
Interior illustrations by Yancey Labat and Steven Lee Stinnett

ISBN 0-439-81431-6

12 11 10 9 8 7 6 5 4 3 2 1   5 6 7 8 9 10/0

Printed in the U.S.A.
First Little Apple printing, September 2005

THE Groovy Girls

TWINS

O'Ryan

BEST FRIENDS

Reese's twin.
Loves to win.

Oki

Adores fashion.
Always looks smashin'.

Yvette

Wannabe star.
Like lightning in a jar.

Reese

Twin number two.
Fab gal
through and through.

BEST FRIENDS

Gwen

Better late than never.
Reese's friend forever.

Vanessa

Great player.
Truth-sayer.

BEST FRIENDS

Chapter 1

PJs by Day: The Thursday Morning Special

"**H**oney on toast with banana smooshed on top is the BEST breakfast ever!" Reese McCloud announced to her twin sister, O'Ryan.

"Nuh-uh," O'Ryan replied, in a just as know-it-all voice. "Chocolate-chip pancakes are totally supreme!"

Hmm...Reese hated to admit it, but her twin had a point. Mom's special pancakes rocked. "Okay. Then honey on toast with banana smooshed on top is the most supreme breakfast we can make by *ourselves*."

"True," O'Ryan nodded, "but I'm seven minutes older, so I'm righter."

"*Puh*-lease," Reese answered. "*Righter* isn't even a word!"

"Oh, yeah? Then what do you call someone who writes books?"

"An author!" Reese said. There was no way she was going to say "writer" and give her sister credit for that one.

That was the way it always was between the McCloud twins. They just liked teasing each other about anything—and everything.

They liked teasing adults even better.

Like their dad.

Like that morning.

It started when Mr. McCloud came into the kitchen. First, he glanced between Reese— munching her toast—and the cuckoo clock, which read 8:25 A.M.

Then he double-checked the time on the microwave: 8:25 A.M.

Then he triple-checked it on his watch: 8:25 A.M.

And *then* he looked back at his seven-minutes- younger daughter, still munching her toast.

All the clocks said the school bus would arrive in *just* five minutes.

Yet there was Reese.

Still sitting at the kitchen table. *Still* dressed in her pajamas—the red ones with leopard-print fur on the collar and cuffs—*still* chewing calmly.

"Reese," Dad said in his I'm-the-dad-and- you're-driving-me-crazy voice. "Get dressed!"

O'Ryan started giggling. Poor Dad, he just didn't get it.

And he hadn't even seen O'Ryan yet, because

she was hidden behind the refrigerator door, looking for her lunch.

But as soon as he heard her laugh, Dad got his *second* shock of the morning.

O'Ryan was still in her jammies, too!

"O'Ryan!" Dad cried out, "you're not dressed yet, either? *Please* tell me you have your school clothes on under that bathrobe!"

"Well, Dad, actually, I *do* have my school clothes on. If you call my PJs school clothes," O'Ryan said, smiling. "Which on Pajama Day you can."

"*What?!*" said Dad.

O'Ryan looked at Reese, and Reese looked at O'Ryan. Even though they were twins, they looked nothing alike. (That was because they were fraternal twins, not identical ones.) But still, they knew *exactly* what the other was thinking: Dad was clueless.

"Pajama Day?" he said, trying to get it straight. "Does your mother know about this?"

"Yup!" O'Ryan answered. "Everyone's supposed to wear their PJs over their clothes today."

"What in the *world* for?" Dad asked.

"So we can learn the stuff that happens at night when everyone's in bed, sleeping," Reese said.

"Or—in your case, Dad—in bed, snoring!" O'Ryan said, imitating his snore. "*Schnuuuh-wee-wee-wee.*"

Dad knocked his fist against his forehead.

The girls knew they had gotten him...again!

Reese laughed, then looked at the clock. "Okay. Time for exit check," she said to O'Ryan.

Like they did every day before leaving the house, the twins marched over to the mirror by the door. Each looked at herself first, then each inspected the other. They did this to make sure they didn't have shirts on inside out, skirts on backward, or flies unzipped. The unzipped zipper was Enemy Number One of the McCloud twins.

It really *was* amazing how different the girls looked. Reese's straight brown hair was perfectly combed and shiny. O'Ryan's very red hair was crazy curly. It barely looked like she had brushed it at all, which—in truth— she hadn't. She *did* brush her teeth, though, and as Dad might say, "That was *no small miracle!*"

"Come on, O'Ryan," Reese said. "Get your rear in gear. We don't want to be late."

O'Ryan narrowed her eyes at her sister.

"For someone who is seven whole minutes *younger* than me, you sure do sound like a pushy older sister."

"Takes one to know one!" Reese said, playfully sticking her tongue out.

"Well then!" O'Ryan replied, taking her seven-minutes-younger sister by the arm. "I guess we should make like cows and *moo*-ve out!"

"Have an *udderly* good day, then," Dad said, trying to get back in the game and keep up with the twin talk at the same time.

"*Moo-cheese*, gracias, Daddy," Reese responded. "And a good night to you, too!"

Chapter 2

School Daze

"Feels like Halloween!" O'Ryan said, looking around the class. It was only the end of September, but Reese knew where her twin was coming from. There was *excitement* in the air. A sense of e-lectricity.

Plus, it helped that everyone was dressed in their jammies.

"Oooh, look at her nightgown!" Reese pointed to a girl in their fourth grade classroom. "And hey, O'Ryan! Check Mike out."

O'Ryan turned to look at Mike. He was wearing a sweet pair of blue-and-white-striped pajamas.

"Your cutie-pie looks a-dorable in his PJs, doesn't he?" Reese smiled.

"What?!" O'Ryan gasped. Her mouth dropped open and her cheeks turned pink. As a redhead, O'Ryan blushed a lot. And when she felt her face get hot, she blushed even more. "*My* cutie-pie? In your dreams, Reese!"

"No, in *your* dreams." Reese giggled.

"That's krazy with a 'k,'" O'Ryan said. "If Oki was here, she'd tell you!" Even though the twins had each other, they, of course, had other friends, too. Oki and O'Ryan had been friends for what seemed like forever. "Oki knows that just because I think Mike is a good goalie—and he happens to be cute—it doesn't mean I 'like him' like him."

"Like *who*?" Oki asked, breezing into class, her anklet jingling, her silk robe blowing behind her.

"No-one-never-mind," O'Ryan said quickly. "Hey, *pizzaz-zy* bathrobe!"

"Thanks!" Oki replied. "But actually, it really isn't a bathrobe. It's a kimono."

"Oh, yeah," O'Ryan said. "That's what I meant. *Pizzaz-zy* kimono!"

"*Domo arigato!*" Oki answered, saying the

Japanese words for "thank you," and giving O'Ryan a big hug.

Oki Omoto was a hugger.

At one point, Oki thought about becoming an air-kisser, too. But she decided air-kissing was fakey-fake, and that was *not* what she was about at all!

"I hope Gwen isn't late again today," Reese said, looking at the clock. She didn't want her friend to get in trouble. Their teacher, Mrs. Pearlman, was big on punctuality.

A few seconds later when Gwen rushed into the classroom, she ran straight to Reese. "Hey, did Mrs. P. ask where I was yet?"

"Nope!" Reese replied. "In fact, you even beat the teacher in this morning."

"For true?"

"No lie," Reese nodded.

"Phewy!" Gwen said, blowing her blond hair off her forehead and doing a little dance for joy. "I told my mom I couldn't be tardy today. I mean, on PJ Day, you can't say you were late 'cause your outfit wasn't working, right?"

When Gwen took off her jacket and revealed her pajamas—red flannel PJs with leopard-print fur on the collar and cuffs, which were exactly the same ones that Reese was wearing—the two girls squealed.

"Su-*preme*," Reese said, pointing to her own PJs. "Same-same!"

"Ohmigosh," Gwen replied. "And we didn't even plan this! I mean, it's like we're *twins* today!"

Hearing the word 'twins,' O'Ryan turned around. Usually, whenever anyone said 'twins,' she was being talked about. But since Gwen and Reese were dressed identically today, Gwen looked more like Reese's sister than O'Ryan did.

"Twins? Oh, *puh*-lease," O'Ryan sniffed. Being a twin was no small deal. O'Ryan thought her sister should have known that. "Hey, Oki," O'Ryan said loudly, "I only have *one* Sweet Tart left—and it's a yellow one—want it?"

O'Ryan always carried a roll of Sweet Tarts, since they were her favorite candy. She loved all the flavors—and their pastel colors, too. But, since Reese only liked the yellow ones, O'Ryan usually gave them to her.

"Thanks!" Oki answered, popping the candy in her mouth.

But before Reese could say anything like, "Um, *hello? I'm* the one who always gets your lemony Sweet Tarts!" the classroom door swung open and everyone ran for their desks.

Mrs. Pearlman had arrived.

"Good morning, Mrs. Pearlman," Reese said.

"I think you mean 'Good night,' don't you, Reese?" Mrs. Pearlman smiled. "It's Pajama Day after all!" (That was part of Mrs. P.'s greatness. She totally got into things.) "Now, since we're going to be learning about the night sky, I need some volunteers to help set the mood."

When Mrs. Pearlman saw Gwen at her desk with her hand up, she smiled again. "Why Gwen, what a lovely surprise to see you here so early!"

"Thank you, Mrs. Pearlman," Gwen replied, "but no one is more surprised than me!" She was a girl who was very used to being kidded about her *"late-i-tude."*

"You can close the blinds, Gwen," Mrs. Pearlman said. "And Mike, turn out the lights, if you would. I'd like the rest of you to look up at the ceiling."

At the mention of Mike's name, Reese turned to her twin and made a little kissy noise.

"Rubber-glue," O'Ryan replied. "Bounces off me and sticks to you!"

When Mike turned out the lights, the whole class started making an *oohing* sound.

"Neat, huh?" Mrs. Pearlman asked. She'd put glow-in-the-dark stars all over the ceiling. "That's our galaxy, and the stars up there are arranged in patterns called constellations."

"Hey, that's Orion's belt," Gwen called out, pointing at the three stars placed directly in a row.

"My *what*?" O'Ryan said, hearing her name.

"Orion. Not O'Ryan, O'Ryan. O-R-I-O-N, not O-R-Y-A-N," Gwen repeated. "Get it?"

No.

O'Ryan had *no* clue what Gwen was talking about. But she knew she didn't like all the fuss about her unusual name. O'Ryan had been given her mother's maiden name (her last name before she married). Most days, she thought this was pretty cool. But sometimes she thought it would have been even cooler if her mom's last name had been "Jennifer" or "Ashley" instead. It would have made finding name bracelets a *lot* easier!

"See?" Gwen explained. "There's a constellation called Orion, and the three stars make up his belt."

"So what you're saying is that Orion is a superstar with great accessories!" Oki responded excitedly.

Now *that* was something O'Ryan could relate to!

"I guess that makes me a superstar, too!" O'Ryan exclaimed happily.

"More like a space cadet, if you ask me," Reese replied.

The class continued to talk about the night sky, but Reese started thinking about something else.

For the rest of the "evening," she couldn't help wondering why her parents had named her sister after something as *pizzaz-zy* as a star. It didn't seem fair.

But as soon as her stomach started rumbling for lunch, it came to her.

Her parents had named her after something even *better*: They'd named her after a peanut butter cup!

Of course, Reese wasn't sure she'd been named for Reese's Peanut Butter Cups, but she *knew* her parents loved both peanut butter and chocolate. And *that*, in Reese's opinion, was supremely sweet!

The only thing sweeter at the moment was the sound of the lunch bell!

BRRRING!

Chapter 3

When Fries Fly

"**S**tewed mush with a side of brown goop,"
Reese said when she and Gwen got in the lunch
line. "Bet that's what we're having today." This was
a pretty good guess when it came to cafeteria food.

But the girls were pleasantly surprised by the
special PJ Day meal: A scoop of "moon" tuna, flying
saucer-shaped Tater Tots, chicken-and-stars soup,
"berry tired" fruit cup, and an Oreo Dream Bar.

"Not bad for the hairnet squad!" Gwen said
when she saw the lunch menu.

Oki and O'Ryan were brown-bag bringers, but
Reese and Gwen bought lunch every day. Actually,

until Gwen moved to their school last year, Reese had been a bringer, too. But Reese liked going through the lunch line with Gwen. So, despite some really *yucky* lunches, Reese was now a lunch-line buyer, too.

Glancing down the line behind them, Reese spotted Vanessa and Yvette. They were fifth graders who'd been BFF for, like, F.

"Hey!" Reese waved.

"What's up?" Vanessa shouted back. For Pajama Day, she was wearing a purple football jersey dotted with purple rhinestones, and a matching bandanna in her pony-tailed hair. Against her caramel-colored skin, Vanessa's purple outfit looked incredible.

"Supreme jammies, Vanessa!" Reese said.

"Yvette!" Gwen yelled. "Show us what *you're* wearing."

"My PJs were designed by Armani," Yvette replied, twirling around like an actress on the red carpet. "Well, Armani and my mommy." Yvette was very trendy, and she always tried thinking like a celebrity.

"You look *beautilicious*!" said Reese.

"I am *sooooo* hungry," Vanessa groaned, counting the heads in front of her in line. "I need food ASAP!"

"Here, I'll help you out," Gwen shouted back, throwing Vanessa one of her Tater Tots. Gwen then threw another one to Yvette—but Yvette missed it—and the tot plopped to the floor.

Yvette thought about eating it, anyway—after all, it had only been on the ground three seconds. And everyone knew you had at least five seconds before germs attached—that's why it was called the "five-second rule!" But Yvette decided this was *not* something a celeb would do. So she just picked it up and waited to find a trash can.

By then, Gwen and Reese were up to the cashier.

"Almost forgot to get a drink!" Reese said. "I'll meet you at the table." But when Reese got to the cooler, a stern voice stopped her cold.

"Stop and drop the juice box," a lunch lady said. "What, *exactly*, do you think you're doing?"

"Um, getting some juice?" Reese answered.

"I think you have some explaining to do, young lady," the lunch lady replied.

Huh? Why would the cafeteria lady want her to explain why she was getting juice? Maybe her hairnet was on too tight.

"You see…" Reese answered slowly, as though talking to someone who didn't get it, "I was thirsty… so I wanted to buy juice…to drink with my meal."

"I was referring to the food fight you started a few minutes ago," the lunch lady replied.

"*What?*" Reese asked. "I didn't start a food fight!"

"I just saw a girl wearing red flannel pajamas throwing food across the lunch line. Are you calling my eyes liars?"

Oh, no!

Reese didn't know how to answer. She *couldn't* say a girl wearing red flannel pajamas hadn't thrown food. But *she* wasn't the red flannel pajama-girl in question. If she told the lunch lady the truth, Gwen would get in trouble. If not, she was on the hook.

Luckily, Vanessa and Yvette came to the rescue just then. Fifth graders *knew* how to handle things.

"Reese is totally innocent of all charges," Vanessa stated in her most lawyer-like voice.

"But I caught your friend red-handed. I mean red-pajama-shirted," the lunch lady replied.

"Well, if anyone's going to get punished, it should be me," Vanessa said responsibly. "I was the one who couldn't wait to eat."

"I see." The cafeteria lady nodded. "In that case, you can *both* be in trouble."

"Wait, you can't just punish the two of them... 'cause it was my fault, too. Look!" Yvette said, showing the Tater Tot she still held in her hand.

The lunch lady gasped. No, not because of Yvette's Tater Tot. But because, just then, *another* flying saucer whizzed by her head. O'Ryan, Oki, and Gwen waved to them from the direction of the flying Tot.

Having seen what was happening, Oki and O'Ryan had filled Gwen in as soon as she had sat at their table. "We gotta fix this!" Gwen had said.

"I know! We'll distract the lunch lady," Oki had replied, handing O'Ryan a Tater Tot from Gwen's tray. "O'Ryan, you've got good aim, so let 'er rip!"

And rip O'Ryan did!

The good news was, the girls' plan to distract the lunch lady had worked.

The bad news was, quicker than you could say, "to the principal's office!" the lunch lady had marched over to the three seated girls. Vanessa, Yvette, and Reese had followed after her.

"Who threw *this* Tater Tot?" the lunch lady asked.

O'Ryan nodded. "Me," she said.

"Actually, *I* threw it," Oki confessed. "Well, I mean I *would* have thrown it, but I have really bad aim."

"No, this is all *my* fault," Gwen said. "*I* was the one who started the whole thing!"

When the lunch lady looked at Gwen, who was dressed in very familiar-looking red flannel pajamas, she blinked in confusion. *Two girls in the same PJs?* "Wait a second!" she said. "Who really started it?"

"*I* did," Gwen said.

"*I* did," Reese said.

"*I* did," O'Ryan said.

"*I* did," Oki said.

"*I* did," Vanessa said.

"*I* did," Yvette said.

The lunch lady shook her head. "Six against one," she laughed. "I give up." The group had outwitted her, and she knew it.

"If you think about it," Reese said, thinking quickly, "this is all just a big compliment to your cooking. Because your flying-saucer Tater Tots really fly."

The lunch lady tried to hide a smile. "Okay, since today is a special day, I'll choose to believe that," she said. "But no more flying food, okay?" When the girls nodded, the lunch lady turned on her squishy shoes, and walked back to the kitchen.

As soon as the lunch lady was out of sight, the girls started laughing. They couldn't help it.

"That was supreme!" Oki said, taking a big bite out of her peanut butter brown-bag sandwich. "Suchgoodteamwork," she continued, trying to unstick her tongue from the roof of her mouth.

"Huh, what?" Reese asked.

"Something about teamwork," O'Ryan

translated, and Oki tapped her finger to her nose.

"It was 'cause we all hung together that we didn't all hang separately," Yvette added. "Like the song goes, 'That's what friends are for.'"

"Just think of all the trouble we could avoid if we kept this going," O'Ryan added.

Vanessa put her hand in the middle of their circle. "I'm in," she said.

All the girls, one after the other, piled their hands on top of Vanessa's, each repeating, "I'm in!"

Of course, no one had any idea what she was going to be *in* for, but that was part of the fun!

Chapter 4

May the Best Team Win

Your slippers stink," Reese said, fanning her nose as O'Ryan changed shoes.

"Nuh-uh," O'Ryan replied, slipping into her cleats. "It's just that your nose smells!" All six girls were sitting in the bleachers, putting on their soccer gear before practice.

"I wish we could keep our jammies on," Gwen said, unbuttoning the pajama top she had on over her soccer jersey.

"Not me," Oki said, carefully folding her kimono. "I mean, do you know how hard it is to get grass stains out of *silk*?"

"Guess what the coach told me," Vanessa said, standing up to stretch. "Tigers play Hurricanes in practice today." Vanessa was captain of the Tigers, and Reese and Oki were on her team.

O'Ryan, Yvette, and Gwen were on the other team, the Hurricanes.

"Well, too bad you're gonna lose!" O'Ryan teased.

"The only thing I'm gonna *lose*," Vanessa replied, "is *you* when you try to run after me!"

"May the best team win!" Gwen added. Then she whispered to Yvette and O'Ryan, "And by the *best* team, of course I mean *our* team!"

"Let's hustle, Hurricanes," Mike yelled, calling his team to the field. Mike was goalie and captain of the Hurricanes, and he played to win. "O'Ryan, you stay on Vanessa. You're the only one who can keep up with her. Okay?"

"Gotcha," O'Ryan said, quickly looking away. *She* knew she was a good player, but hearing it from Mike was *especially* nice.

"Who should I cover, Mike?" Gwen asked, hoping she'd get a compliment, too.

"Just stay out of O'Ryan's way," Mike replied.

"Hey!" Gwen answered, supremely miffed. She knew she wasn't a soccer star, but that was a *very* un-nice thing to say!

On the other side of the field, Vanessa was

giving a pep talk to her team. "Okay, Tigers, I just want you to go out there and have fun. But," she smiled, "more important than that...I want you to KICK HURRICANE BUTT! Now roar with me."

"ROAR!" the Tigers replied.

When the whistle blew, both teams were called to the field. Vanessa, Oki, and Reese went to one side. Yvette, O'Ryan, and Gwen went to the other. Reese waved to Gwen from her side, and Gwen waved back. Reese was about to wave again, but she saw Vanessa watching her.

"You weren't going to wave to a Hurricane, were you?" Vanessa asked.

"Well," Reese replied, dropping her hands, "I *was* thinking about it."

"Well," Vanessa nodded. "You should *stop* thinking about it. 'Cause when that horn blows, Gwen isn't your friend—she's your opponent. Got it?"

"I guess," Reese replied. But she wasn't sure.

"*Seriously*," Vanessa said, "you owe it to your Tiger teammates to play your hardest—even if that means battling against Gwen. Now ROAR it!"

"Roar," Reese replied, but she could only manage a soft sound.

The captains went to the center of the field for the coin toss. That would decide which team got the ball first.

"Tails!" Vanessa yelled.

"Heads!" Mike answered.

"Yes!" Mike pumped his fist when Heads won. He took the ball from the referee. "Oh, and Vanessa?" Mike said. "Good luck…you're going to need it."

Vanessa squinted her eyes at him. "Prepare to become flat-bread!" she said back.

As soon as the starting whistle blew, the Hurricanes' forward, Jay, kicked the ball to O'Ryan.

The two ran down the field toward the Tigers' goal, picture-perfectly passing the ball between them. But soon enough, they heard footsteps.

Thump. Thump. Thump.

It was Vanessa.

O'Ryan tried to pass. But Vanessa snagged the ball, then quickly reversed direction, running down the field toward the opposite goal.

"Woo-*hoo*!" Oki yelled. "Go, Vanessa!" She liked cheering her teammates and dancing around the field as *much* as she liked running and kicking.

"Where are my Tigers?" Vanessa asked, looking to pass. She soon saw Reese and kicked the ball to her. Reese ran with it for a moment, but Hurricane Gwen soon got in front of her. Seeing her friend, Reese smiled. But suddenly, she remembered the words of her captain: *"Gwen isn't your friend—she's your opponent."*

So Reese knew what she had to do...and Reese the Tiger rammed past Gwen the Hurricane.

Gwen teetered. She tottered. And then she fell down. *Splat!*

But Reese didn't look back. She just stuck with the ball until she could return it to Vanessa.

When Vanessa reconnected, she sent the ball flying. The Hurricanes rushed to stop it.

"Got it!" O'Ryan yelled.

But then she *missed* it.

"Mine!" Yvette called.

But it wasn't even *a little bit* hers.

Instead, the ball continued to soar. It flew back towards the Tigers' goal where Mike was standing.

He looked ready to catch it.

He put out his arms.

He jumped up.

And then...

And then...

He missed it! The ball slipped right through his hands and landed in the back of the net.

"Yes!" Vanessa shouted. "SCORE!"

When the final whistle blew, the score was Tigers 1, Hurricanes 0.

"Nice!" Vanessa shouted to her Tiger team.

"Great job! Now let's line up for the end-of-game handshake."

Being a good sportswoman was part of the game.

"Hey, Vanessa," O'Ryan said, as the two girls high-fived. "Nice shot."

"Thanks, you played great, too," Vanessa replied. "I couldn't believe I got past you!"

"Me, neither," O'Ryan laughed.

"Good game," Reese said when it was her turn to high-five Gwen.

But Gwen didn't reply "good game." Instead, she just stared at Reese for a moment. "You knocked me down," she said finally.

"But," Reese replied, feeling terrible, "I totally didn't mean to. See, Vanessa said I had to think of you as my opponent. And I didn't want to. And I'm sorry. Please don't be mad, okay?"

"Well…" Gwen replied, still looking annoyed.

"I'm *really* sorry," Reese said.

"Okay," Gwen nodded, "I'll forgive ya—this time." That was one of the great things about Gwen. She could never stay mad for very long. "But boy-oh-boy," Gwen said, "I sure wish Vanessa had been on my team!"

"How's that?" Mike asked, overhearing Gwen. "Why would you want Vanessa on our team?"

"Um…maybe because she just happens to be awesome," Oki replied, getting into the conversation.

"Yeah, right!" Mike snorted.

The other girls gathered around.

"Besides, Vanessa's faster, smarter, *and* taller than you," Gwen responded. She still hadn't quite forgiven Mike for telling her to stay out of the way earlier.

"Well," Vanessa said, joining in. "I can do anything as long as my friends help me."

"Like when we were so supreme in the cafeteria today," O'Ryan added.

"And we totally *did* stay out of trouble the whole rest of the day," Reese said.

"You mean the whole rest of the *night*!" Yvette corrected.

Mike shook his head. "You girls are all talk! I bet you couldn't *really* stay up all night. You'd probably fall asleep before midnight."

"Oh, yeah? If that's a challenge, you're on!" Vanessa replied. "We'll even bet you we can stay up *all* night."

"Okay, it's a bet then," Mike nodded.

But the girls knew this was no ordinary bet. This was going to be a supreme challenge!

Chapter 5

A Big Mess

"**S**o we're going to have a no-sleep sleepover. Get it, Mom?" O'Ryan said, explaining the bet.

"Tell me *again* why it *has* to be at *our* house?" Mom asked, not getting it at all.

"We need to prove to Mike we stayed awake all night," Reese replied.

The girls had just gotten back from soccer practice and were still keyed up.

"And since he lives across the street," O'Ryan said, "he can check up on us to make sure we aren't cheating."

"Oh," Mom nodded. "Well, I think a sleepover is a fun idea, but—"

There was always a *"but."*

"But—quiet time starts at 11:30 P.M. And, if you want to have it here, you're going to have to clean up your room, too."

O'Ryan ran her hand through her curly red hair. She knew Mom wasn't talking about Reese's half of their room. Reese's half was always neat.

"*C'mon*, Mom," O'Ryan said. "Cleaning up is silly. I mean, why should I make my bed in the morning if I'm only going to sleep in it again at night?"

"O'Ryan," Mom replied, "your side of the room is so messy, it would make a garbage collector cry."

"But *Mom*," O'Ryan pleaded.

"But *O'Ryan*," Mom imitated. "You know I love you just the way you are. But the girls will need space on the floor for their sleeping bags. So, just for the party, try to make your side look like Reese's, okay?"

"O-kay," O'Ryan agreed and started thinking about how *little* cleaning she could get away with!

But it was still only Thursday, and the party wasn't until Saturday. No need to sweat it now.

At 6:15 P.M. on Saturday, O'Ryan walked into her room to begin cleaning up.

And at 6:16 P.M., she tripped over a fuzzy-haired

angel doll that was lying on the carpet. O'Ryan had 31 dolls in her "all things angel" collection, most of which were on the floor. Reese had 33 items in her "butterfly stuff" collection. But Reese's things were in a neat shoebox.

Even Reese's pink-and-white desk was neat, with her diary sitting on top of a tidy stack of books.

"Spam!" O'Ryan shouted in frustration.

But all of a sudden—as one of her boots toppled off the shoe rack in her closet—it hit her.

No, not the boot.

The perfect solution!

Mom wanted O'Ryan's half of the room to "look like Reese's." O'Ryan realized she might never get her half of the room as neat as her sister's. *BUT* she *could* make her sister's half as messy as hers!

"*G-een-ius!*" O'Ryan exclaimed.

She started rumpling Reese's bed. She kicked Reese's shoes out of order. She knocked over some books on her twin's desk. O'Ryan didn't mean for *all* of Reese's books to go tumbling. But they did.

Things got pretty messy pretty fast.

Too messy, almost—even for her.

So O'Ryan bent down to pick up some books. That's when she saw Reese's diary—on the floor— open to the entry from two days ago. And before O'Ryan even realized what she was doing, her eyes had skimmed the first few lines.

Thursday

Dear Diary, ❈

Today at school was super-supreme! Everybody wore their pajamas to school (because it was Pajama Day, Diary, not because everyone forgot to change into regular clothes!). ✦

O'Ryan smiled, thinking she would have written exactly the same thing.

I wore my favorite red PJs and guess what? ✦
Gwen wore exactly the same thing, too! I don't think wearing the same jammies makes you twins, but I do think it probably makes us BFF. Anyway, I hope it means we're Best Friends Forever because I think Gwen is totally supreme! ❈

"Best friends?" O'Ryan said aloud. O'Ryan thought *she* was her twin's best friend.

"Who you talking to?" Reese asked, as she walked into the room. "*Sheesh*-kabob! What happened in here?"

O'Ryan started to explain. "See, Mom said both sides of our rooms should look alike, so—"

But then Reese saw the diary—*her* diary—in her sister's hands.

"Wait a minute, is that *MY* diary?" Reese asked, her voice suddenly getting higher.

"Well, I was just..." O'Ryan sputtered, not knowing what to say next.

"That's PRIVATE!" Reese yelled, snatching her book away.

"I didn't mean to read it!" O'Ryan yelled back.

"You invaded my privacy!" Reese said.

"You shouldn't have kept it out where it could fall open and I could read it!" O'Ryan answered.

"I'm gonna tell Mom!" Reese said, running down the stairs.

"Or you could go cry to your *best friend* Gwen about it!" O'Ryan replied, chasing after her.

But just as the girls got to the bottom of the steps, the doorbell rang. Hearing the noise, Mom came into the entryway.

"Girls," she said, "what's the fuss?"

Both twins started talking at the same time.

"Hold on! Time-out!" Mom said. "Your friends are here, so *now* is not the time for fighting. You can deal with it later. But it stops now. Got it?"

"*But—*" Reese started to say. But when she looked at her mother, she kept the rest of the thought to herself.

"Now, how does your room look, O'Ryan?" Mom asked.

"My side looks like Reese's," O'Ryan replied. But for some reason, O'Ryan no longer thought the "*g-een-ius*" solution she'd come up with earlier seemed quite so clever anymore.

Chapter 6

Saturday Night Live: Get This Party Started!

makeover

"I know I'm *so* early," Oki said at 7 P.M. "But I came now 'cause I thought O'Ryan 'might' need some help cleaning her room." Oki used finger quotes around the word "might."

"That's very nice of you, Oki," Mom laughed.

"I can also help Reese style her outfit or something, if she wants," Oki quickly added.

"Oki, you are queen-supreme," O'Ryan said.

"You think?" Oki giggled, hopping up the stairs. "You coming, Reese?"

"Nope. I'm just going to make sure everything's ready down here," Reese replied. It was nice of Oki to ask, but she'd had enough of O'Ryan for a while.

Reese stood there for a moment, hoping Gwen would arrive soon. But just like you could always count on Oki to be early, you could always count on Gwen to be late!

Before they knew it, it was 7:30 P.M., and Vanessa and Yvette had arrived.

"Girls," Vanessa said, entering the McCloud house, "are we ready or what?"

There was only one right answer. "YES!"

"Good," Yvette nodded. "'Cause this is going to be *waaaaay* fun!"

"Hey, what's in the box, Vanessa?" O'Ryan asked.

"In this case is something no sleepover party should be without." Vanessa flipped open the locks to reveal three levels of eye shadow, lip gloss, glitter pots, and blush.

There was much *oohing* and *ahhing*.

"Thank you, thank you, thank you!" Gwen said from the other side of the screen door. She'd just arrived, and pretended the girls were *oohing* and *ahhing* over her.

"Gwen!" Reese said excitedly, "Come in! Vanessa was just showing us her makeup case."

"Cool! I *heart* makeup!" Gwen said. "But my mom never lets me buy any of my own."

"Mine, neither," Vanessa smiled. "That's why I brought her stuff!"

Because Vanessa was the oldest at the party, she thought it was her job to share what she knew with the younger girls. For instance, she knew that to stay awake all night, things had to be kept exciting. So she had told the girls in advance to think of three party games each and write them down. Later, at the twins' house, they'd throw the ideas in a hat to pick and play at random during the night.

"But wait…" Yvette said, "there's more!" From behind her back, she revealed a bag from a cheese shop.

"You brought cheese?" Oki asked, wrinkling her nose.

"*As if*," Yvette replied. "But to do one of my ideas, I needed to bring—"

"Wait!" Gwen yelled. "Don't tell us. We want to keep it a surprise, right?" She took a beautiful black top hat out of one of her shopping bags, and the girls tossed in their suggestions. "Reese, you go first, since you're the hostess with the mostest," Gwen said. Then, looking at O'Ryan, she quickly added, "I mean *you're* the hostess, too, O'Ryan, but, um…someone has to go first."

"Okay," Reese said, reaching her hand in the hat. She picked a slip and read it: "Time to make Rice Krispies Treats!"

"Hot dog!" Vanessa turned to Yvette. "That one has to be yours, right?"

"You are correct!" Yvette replied. "I have all the ingredients right here in my stinky cheese bag!"

"*Woo-hoo!*" Oki shouted. "I love Rice Krispies Treats, but I haven't been allowed to make them since *the accident.*"

"What accident?" O'Ryan asked.

"The accident where I fed a couple to my cat. Nothing *too-too* bad happened. But his stomach snapped, crackled, and popped for the rest of the night!"

"Note to self," Yvette said. "Oki does *not* take home extra Rice Krispies Treats."

The girls laughed, and ran to the kitchen to start

the great mini-marshmallow-melting feast. Mom melted the butter and mixed in the marshmallows. Then the girls started adding the Rice Krispies and the other special ingredients Yvette had brought, including Reese's Pieces (in honor of Reese!).

The hard part, of course, was waiting until the treats were cool enough to eat.

While they waited, Oki reached into the hat. "Ready for this?" she asked, unfolding the paper. "Says here..." Oki paused and narrowed her eyes as she looked between the girls, "PILLOW FIGHT!"

As soon as the words left her mouth, Oki ran out of the kitchen.

She sprinted up the stairs and grabbed her pillow in the twins' room. The rest of the girls tried to catch up to her, but by the time they got upstairs, Oki was already swinging.

Oki, it turned out, was a pillow-fighting machine!

Thwomp!

Whack!

Ka-pow!

Yelps, giggles, and feathers flew.

"Oh, Yvette!" Vanessa called out.

Yvette turned around...MISTAKE! She looked

toward Vanessa, but all she saw was a big pillow coming at her. "Pretty sneaky!" Yvette laughed, crashing onto O'Ryan's bed. Then, getting up a moment later, Yvette said, "Oh! Wait, Vanessa—?"

"Yeah?" Vanessa turned back around.

"This is what we call payback, baby!" Yvette raised her pillow above her head.

Wallop-arooni!

More yelps.

More giggles.

More feathers went flying.

Finally, Gwen plopped on Reese's bed. "Oh, man," she said, "I'm zonked."

"You know what?" Reese replied, fanning herself, her heart beating fast. "We should stop, 'cause we need to stay strong."

The girls stopped the bopping and looked at the clock. It was only 9:30 P.M. Only two hours had passed since the party started, and they had a long night ahead. But when the doorbell rang a little while later, they were back on their feet, running down the stairs.

They knew the sound of that bell meant food.

"Pizza! Pizza!" Yvette yelled.

"Dad! Delivery dude's here!" O'Ryan called out.

As they waited for Mr. McCloud to come to the door, Gwen said, "Brainstorm! The pizza guy works all night long, right?"

"Yeah," Vanessa agreed. "So?"

"So I bet he could give us some tips on how to stay awake till morning."

"Smart!" Reese responded, covering her mouth to stop her yawn.

"Veggie Supreme, right?" the pizza guy asked, when Dad opened the door.

"*Very* supreme," O'Ryan replied.

"So," Gwen said, stepping forward. "What kind of pizza do most people order when they're trying to stay awake all night?"

The delivery guy smiled. "Well, the Meat-Lover's Pizza will keep you awake for hours."

"And how!" Dad laughed. "I've had a few long nights with that pizza myself."

"Oh, I have a question!" Vanessa said.

"Me too, me too," Oki added.

"Listen, girls," Dad interrupted, "I bet there are a lot of hungry people out there waiting for this man."

"Yeah," the pizza guy nodded, "I *do* have to make a delivery to the Wellstones across the street.

But I guess I have time for one more question."

"Okay, why aren't there delivery-boy *girls*?" Vanessa asked.

"Well, I don't really know the answer to that," he laughed. "Although, if any of you are looking for a job, all you need is a driver's license."

"Sure," Gwen replied, "*and* the ability *not* to eat the pizzas!"

Reese carried the giant pizza box upstairs and handed out the slices.

"Ready Freddies?" Yvette said, breaking a string of cheese hanging off her slice. She reached into the hat for the next activity. "Interesting," she nodded. "So when the guy said he was delivering a pizza to the Wellstones across the street, he meant *Mike Wellstone*, right?"

"Probably," Reese said with a playful smile. "Mike likes pizza, doesn't he, O'Ryan?"

O'Ryan got that crazy butterfly feeling in her stomach. "How am I supposed to know that?" O'Ryan replied quickly. "Anyway, why would I care?"

"Because," Yvette replied, "written on this slip of paper, it says our next game is 'Spy on Mike.'"

Chapter 7

Nothing but the Truth...or Dare

"So, are you guys ready for some Mike-time detective work?" Vanessa asked, finishing her pizza.

"Definitely," Reese said, with a playful smile. "I think that sounds like a great idea!"

All the girls nodded and giggled.

Well, *almost* all the girls, that is...everyone, except O'Ryan.

"No!" O'Ryan yelped. "I mean, we need to wait before we go spying. Because..."

The girls looked at O'Ryan. *Because* why?

O'Ryan needed a reason. She couldn't say she and Mike were *sort of* friends. She couldn't admit that if Mike caught her spying, he might never like her again.

"...*Because* if we don't wait, we won't digest our food properly." O'Ryan smiled weakly. She was hoping that if they put off spying, the girls might forget about it entirely.

"I've heard that," Oki nodded. "Like my grandma always says, you're supposed to wait for an hour after you've eaten to go swimming, right?"

"Oh, right," Vanessa said. She didn't want anyone to think she'd forgotten such an important sleepover rule (even though she'd never heard of it before).

"So okay, pick something else!" O'Ryan said.

Yvette reached back into the hat. She read the slip. "A-ha! An oldie but goodie," she said, her eyes widening. "Truth or Dare!"

Oh-boy.

Truthfully, as soon as Yvette said those three little words, everyone got a little jittery. Sure, they were all good friends.

But *everyone* had secrets.

"I'll go first," Gwen volunteered, wanting to get her turn out of the way.

"Okay," Yvette replied. "Truth or Dare?"

"Dare," Gwen answered, hoping to avoid the truth.

"Run up and down the steps twenty-five times," Yvette said.

"For real?" Gwen asked.

"Or," Yvette replied, "you could just slide down the steps on your rear twenty-five times instead."

"That's better," Gwen smiled. Planting her tush on the top step, she shoved off. "Here I go!"

Bump. Bump. Bump. Bump. Bump. Bump.
There was a *whole* lot of bumping going on.

When Gwen was finally done, Reese put a pillow on the floor for Gwen to rest her sore behind on.

The Truth or Dare rule was: "She Who Dares Last, Dares Next." So next up was Yvette. "Dare," Yvette said boldly.

"I think yours should involve a song," O'Ryan said.

Everyone nodded. Yvette loved music, so this seemed perfect.

"I dare you," O'Ryan continued, "to sing and do the chicken dance."

"Ha!" Yvette laughed. "Child's play." She was a natural performer.

> ♪ *"Dah Dah Dah Dah Dah Dah Dah*
> *da da da da da da da*
> *Dah Dah Dah Dah,*
> *clap clap clap clap"*

She sang and chicken-danced to the beat of her own drumstick. And when she finished, Yvette bowed deeply to the applause of her friends.

"Uh, thank you, thank you very much," Yvette said. "And now, O'Ryan, I believe it's your turn."

"Right," O'Ryan said, jumping up from the circle and dancing around. "Ooh, I feel good! Dare me!"

"Well I'm glad *you're* feeling good," Reese said, turning to her twin. "Because it sounds like you're ready for a mission then."

When O'Ryan looked at her sister, her stomach knotted again.

Reese had that sly look in her eye. It was a look that said, "I haven't forgotten that you read my diary."

"I dare you," Reese said, "to ding-dong-ditch Mike's house."

Oh-boy! This was the worst.

Ringing someone's doorbell—the ding-dong part—then running away—the ditch part—wasn't something O'Ryan had done in a *loooong* time. And it wasn't something she wanted to do tonight.

Especially not *that* doorbell.

"Ding-dong-ditching is so babyish," O'Ryan said. She hoped that by calling it babyish, it would sound uncool enough to be dropped.

"I don't think it's babyish," Gwen replied. "I think it's pretty funny. Plus, that'll prove to Mike we're still awake."

"Thank you," Reese nodded to her friend.

O'Ryan rolled her eyes. *Of course* Gwen would stick up for Reese.

O'Ryan was stuck. She would run *as fast as she possibly could*. The thought of getting caught by Mike was too-too-too awful to even think about.

But, of course, she'd already started thinking about it. O'Ryan pictured having to wear a paper bag over her head to future soccer practices. Or maybe she could just move to a different school.

The girls put on their shoes, and walked downstairs.

Oki looked at O'Ryan. "Don't worry," she whispered. "He'll never know it's you." She squeezed O'Ryan's hand, then said, "But run fast!"

O'Ryan nodded back. "Okay, I'm a go-go ghost." She then sprinted across the street and onto Mike's doorstep. In a window next to the door, she saw the bluish light of a TV in the living room.

O'Ryan glanced back and saw her friends watching her. So she slowly reached her finger toward the doorbell.

As she was about to press the ding-dong, she looked through the window again.

Aahhhh!

Mike!!!

Right there on the living room couch!

O'Ryan dropped to her knees to get out of sight. Then her face scrunched into a question mark, as she thought about what she'd just seen. "Wait a second," she said, slowly rising and peeking back in the window.

There was Mike—fast asleep!

"Beautilicious!" she exclaimed to herself.

O'Ryan quietly creeped off the porch, then jogged back over to her friends.

"What happened?" Vanessa asked.

"You are *so* not going to believe this!" O'Ryan reported.

"Did you ring the bell?" Reese asked. "If not, you didn't do the dare!"

"No, I didn't ring the doorbell. But ask me why!" O'Ryan replied.

"Why?" Oki asked.

"Because if I had, Mike would have woken up!"

"What?"

"Big, strong 'I-can-beat-you-girls' Mike—sleeping like a baby?" Yvette teased. "You're serious?"

"As serious as a bad haircut," O'Ryan replied.

"That's hee-hee-hee-larious!" Oki laughed. "He didn't even make it till midnight!"

"Too bad he doesn't have a great team of girlfriends to help him stay awake!" Gwen said.

"And it's even *more* too bad that this team of girlfriends won't ever let him forget it!" Vanessa added, as the girls went back inside.

"Know what? I don't think we'll be able to outdo that dare," Oki said. So she pulled another slip of paper from the hat. "Makeover time!"

Yvette, Gwen, and Reese gathered around Vanessa, as she popped open the makeup case. But Oki scooted over to O'Ryan and squeezed her arm. "Good work," she said, "and if Mike ever asks any questions, don't worry, I've got you covered."

O'Ryan smiled at her friend.

Then Oki started smearing makeup all over O'Ryan's face—but O'Ryan didn't mind one bit.

Chapter 8

Wake Up and Make Up

"**G**irls, we blew it!" O'Ryan said, rubbing the glitter out of her eyes at 8 A.M. the next morning.

"Keep it down," Gwen yawned. "I'm trying to sleep here!"

"No *duh*," O'Ryan replied. "We were *all* sleeping!"

Vanessa's eyes snapped open.

Yvette sat up.

Oki took off the terry cloth headband that kept the bangs off her face.

Reese looked at O'Ryan, and O'Ryan looked at Reese. And in this "just waking-up" stage, the twins were thinking alike.

"Spam!" they said together, realizing that, even with teamwork, they hadn't stayed awake all night.

"How did this happen?" Vanessa asked. "Last thing I remember, I was closing my eyes—but only so Yvette could put eye shadow on me."

"*Oh*," Yvette replied, "I thought *I* was supposed to close my eyes so *you* could give *me* eye shadow."

"And *I* thought Reese was going to give me a head massage," Gwen said.

"I thought *you* were going to be braiding my hair," Reese responded.

Oki and O'Ryan just shrugged. Neither one of them could remember *how or why* they ended up in their sleeping bags.

Vanessa, the unofficial captain of the slumber party dream team, was crushed. "Man, I'm so bummed. I need to brush my teeth," she said.

"Me too," Yvette replied.

"Me three," Oki nodded.

O'Ryan was bummed, too. But that didn't make her want to brush her teeth. The girls shuffled into the bathroom together. While some brushed, others scrubbed, trying to remove the makeup that had smeared on their faces while they were sleeping.

"Hey, ladies!" Mom called out from downstairs. "Anyone up for some chocolate-chip pancakes?"

That was a question that didn't need to be asked twice. The girls bolted for the stairs.

The pancakes smelled yummy.

They looked even better.

Deee-licious!

Vanessa looked at the girls and said, "I don't think we deserve these. After all, we didn't stay up all night."

"True," Reese said, "but it *would* be kind of a waste to throw them out."

"Waste is bad," Yvette agreed. "There are a lot of starving children out there."

"Like me!" Oki said, softly.

"If you think about it," O'Ryan replied, "we all *did* stay up later than we ever did before."

"And we all *did* stay up later than Mike," Gwen pointed out.

"So I guess we *did* sort of win," Vanessa nodded.

"Maybe we just need to practice staying awake more. And work on our teamwork," Reese added.

"Right!" O'Ryan exclaimed. "Even the *best* teams need practice."

"So that means more no-sleep sleepovers!" Oki said.

"So *that* means we should eat these pancakes before they get cold," Gwen added.

The girls nodded, very happy with their decision. Then they each took a few pancakes and passed around the bag of chocolate chips to sprinkle some more on top. But instead of just putting the chips all over, Oki made hers into an "O" shape.

"Cool, O for Oki! I'm going to make an O for O'Ryan," O'Ryan said, placing her O next to Oki's.

Reese, who was sitting on the other side of Oki and O'Ryan, made an R. Gwen, who was sitting next to Reese, made a G. And Vanessa and Yvette, who were sitting on the other side of Oki and O'Ryan, made a V and a Y.

When O'Ryan looked at the chocolate-chip letters, her mouth dropped open. "Wow!" she said, pointing. "Look! We're G-R-O-O-V-Y."

"Groovy?" Yvette asked.

"You know, hip, hot, cool, stylin'!" O'Ryan said.

"That's sooo waaay cool," Gwen said.

"That's sooo waaay *Groovy*!" O'Ryan corrected.

"And that means..." Vanessa paused, leaning forward to make sure everyone was listening, "we Groovy Girls are a supreme team!"

"And *that* means we'll definitely stay awake at our next no-sleep sleepover," Gwen added.

"Or the one after that," Yvette said.

"Or the one after that," Reese repeated.

O'Ryan put her hand in the middle of the table. "Groovy Girls Forever," she said. The other girls piled their hands on top of hers and beamed.

"Now let's make like archaeologists and dig in!" Reese said—and all the Groovy Girls did.

A little while later, the parents of the Groovy Girls began arriving to pick up their daughters. But even after the last girl (Gwen) left, the twins continued sitting together at the table in their PJs.

It was just like they'd done at the start of Pajama Day on Thursday.

Both wanted to discuss everything that had gone on in the past day. Both wanted to talk about the fight they'd had—even though now it seemed like ages ago. But since neither was exactly sure *what* to say, or *how* to say it, both just sat there. Not talking.

Finally, O'Ryan turned to Reese. "I didn't mean to read your diary. But I'm really sorry I did."

"I know. And I'm sorry I sent you to Mike's," Reese admitted.

"I'm over it now," O'Ryan nodded, "especially since it turned out the way it did." Then she added, "You know, I'm really glad you're such good friends with Gwen. And if she's your best friend, I can understand why, 'cause she's supreme."

"So is Oki," Reese replied. "It's funny. I mean, I always thought you thought of Oki as your best friend. That's why I was so happy when Gwen moved to our school. I wanted a friend like that, too."

O'Ryan had never thought about her friendship with Oki like that. But Reese was right. They'd always *had* what Reese and Gwen now shared. But even though she and her twin had different "best friends," O'Ryan felt pretty sure it didn't change anything between them. Turned out, Reese was having the *identical* twin thought.

They'd always be BTF. Best Twins Forever.

Pajama Party Packing List
from Head to Toe

How to Host the Best
SLUMBER PARTY
Games, Activities, Munchies, and More

Sleepover Q & A's—
SOLVED

Contents

"A Groovy Greeting" by Robin Epstein
Text by Julia Marsden
Illustrations by Jane Archer, Yancey Labat, and Steven Lee Stinnett

A Groovy Greeting

For the first Groovy Girls handbook ever, O'Ryan and Reese share their feelings on sleepovers, friendship, and how to make a good party slumberrific.

Groovy Girls Handbook: What do you like best about slumber parties?

REESE: The beginning part is my fave. Everyone's all excited, but no one knows exactly what's to come. Ya know?

O'RYAN: Well, I love having my friends around. Something funny always happens.

GG: What's the best way to prepare for a party?

REESE: Get lots of sleep before.

O'RYAN: Try to be super-sweet to your mom so she definitely lets you go. Or—so she'll let you host the party.

GG: Are you ever nervous before going to a sleepover? Ever feel like once you get there, you'd rather be home?

O'RYAN: Sometimes, sure. But the thing to remember is that you'll be there with all your friends.

REESE: I think it also helps to know some info beforehand— like what you'll be eating and when you're going to be picked up by your 'rents the next morning. The more I know, the better I feel.

O'RYAN: That's why this handbook rocks. It'll totally give you the 4-1-1.

REESE: And we know it'll help you plan for a supremely groovy sleepover—whether you're throwing one or going to one! So, have fun!

O'RYAN: And remember, be groovy, girls!

Love,
Reese + O'Ryan McCloud
Groovy Girls 4-ever!

The Groovy Girls Sleepover Suitcase

Packing for a pajama party?

Whether it's your first overnight adventure at a friend's, or you've been to a bunch of pajama parties with your pals already, you'll need the lowdown on what to add to your bag for around-the-clock fun and comfort!

As you're throwing stuff into your overnighter, use a head-to-toe suitcase-stuffing strategy. Here are some specifics:

First, start with your head. You definitely don't want bedhead in the morning, so take your favorite comb and/or brush, and a headband or some scrunchies, for that morning mane!

But don't stop with what you need for your hair—what else do you need from the neck up? Your toothbrush, your favorite toothpaste, and anything you've been ordered to wear by an orthodontist.

When it comes to a winning wardrobe for your trip to Slumberland, think options. While your favorite and most stylish jammies are a great choice, you might also want to pack a pair of sweats and a sweatshirt (or hoodie), in case the place where you'll be sleeping is chillier than what you're used to at home.

Sweats also come in handy in the morning as an alternate outfit, if you don't feel comfortable wearing your jammies while joining everyone in the family for breakfast. And, don't forget to bring along some slippers or a pair of socks to avoid popsicle toes!

Make Room for Your Manners!

From the minute you arrive, until the moment you leave, there's something you'll want to have on hand at all times…good manners. How *do* you pack politeness? Here are some do's and don'ts!

DON'T dump your stuff at the door as soon as you enter your friend's house. Ask where you should put your things.

DO act friendly with all members of the household…that includes your friend's pesky little brother!

DON'T wander around on your own. Some areas of the house are likely to be off-limits (like the parents' bedroom and bathroom, and the home office). Also, no opening drawers, closets, or cupboards!

DON'T raid the fridge for snacks. Instead, let your friend know when you're hungry.

DO turn to your pal or her folks if you're feeling homesick or scared. Minding your manners doesn't mean you have to pretend you're okay, if you're not. A phone call home to hear some reassuring words from your mom or dad, or simply to touch base and say "good night," may be all you need to feel more comfortable. Or, you may want to spend the night in your own bed, and then return in the morning to be part of the breakfast brigade. Keep in mind, the whole point of a sleepover is to have fun—not to feel frightened or frazzled.

5

DO pitch in with picking things up the morning after your big bash.

DO say thank you to your friend and to the adults in her family who helped make the sleepover happen.

Check Out This Checklist!

Here's a list that will help you pack perfectly!

- A favorite pillow (a touch of home)
  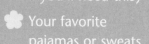

- A sleeping bag (ask your friend if you'll need this)

- Your favorite pajamas or sweats

- Warm socks or slippers

- Comfy clothes to wear in the A.M.

- Toothbrush

- Toothpaste

- Orthodontic stuff

- Lotion

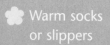

- Lip balm

- Comb and/or brush
  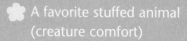

- Headband, hair clips, and/or scrunchies

- A favorite book or magazine

- A favorite stuffed animal (creature comfort)

- Personal stereo and headphones

- A few of your favorite CDs

- Camera and film (memory-making materials)

- Some snacks like a granola bar

- A small flashlight

Your Biggest Sleepover Questions— SOLVED!

Friends and Fighting

My cousin had a birthday sleepover, and two of her guests started arguing. That practically ruined the party. What should I do if something like that happens at my sleepover?

Odds are everyone will get along just great—after all, they're all buds, right? However, if things do get a bit edgy between guests, it's important for you to keep your cool. Remind them that you invited everyone to celebrate the fun of friendship, not to start battles between buds. And be *sure* to avoid taking sides.

Time Out

I went to a sleepover where we were together the entire time. By the next morning, everyone was getting on each other's nerves. How can I avoid this at my next sleepover?

There's definitely such a thing as too much togetherness, even among the best of buds. So, when you plan your next sleepover, be sure to have a few activities that can be done alone.

Set out some nail polish for manicure sessions that can take place with pals or solo. Have some magazines for flipping through, and maybe even a couple of disposable cameras for pic-taking. Also, do any of your friends—like Groovy Girl Yvette—like to cook? Perhaps they can help get things ready in the kitchen. There are lots of ways friends can be part of the party scene and yet still have time for time-out.

Your PERFECT Slumber Party

Hosting a sleepover is super-fun and can be super-easy! All you need are your closest pals, a variety of fun activities (that everyone helps plan), and a parent to help with the details.

One Week Before the Party

* Go over food ideas with your grown-up. Will you order a pizza? Serve up your mom's famous spaghetti? Munch on popcorn at midnight? Chat about tasty treats and meals for the night of the sleepover, and for the next morning.

* Like the Groovy Girls, everyone has creative and fun ideas, and can help plan the sleepover activities. Have each guest think up 2 to 3 party ideas, and bring supplies for those activities, if needed.

* Come up with *your* 2 to 3 party ideas, and get the materials together.

makeover

Week of the Party

* Make sure your parent has all the food together.
* Decide on an area for games, activities, and sleeping, and make sure the house is clean by party time.
* Gather together your fave music to play during the party.

8

As Guests Arrive

✳ Greet your friends and make them feel welcome.

✳ Write down the phone, cell, and/or pager numbers where parents can be reached.

✳ Have fun!

Party Central Checklist!

Here's a party-planning list to review with your folks!

✳ How many friends can you invite?

✳ Where will your guests sleep?

✳ What's on the menu?

✳ Should you ask your friends to bring their own sleeping bags and pillows?

✳ Will you need to rearrange furniture or move stuff to make sure your guests are safe and comfortable?

✳ What rooms are off-limits?

✳ What time is lights out?

✳ Does anyone have a food allergy or special dietary needs?

✳ Should your pet(s) be kept out of the party area due to a guest's allergies or fears?

Throw Your Own
GROOVY GIRLS
Sleepover

You can host a sleepover just as cool as the Groovy Girls! Here's how:

10 Terrific Slumber Party Activities

1. Get up and boogie!
2. **Create a slambook (see page 11).**
3. Get cooking in the kitchen—maybe make some Marshmallow Munchies, just like the Groovy Girls do at their sleepover (see the recipe on page 12).
4. **Take photos of your guests.**
5. Build a fort out of blankets, sleeping bags, and pillows.
6. **Get creative! Arts and crafts are a great party pleaser.**
7. Challenge your friends to a game of Truth or Dare. Guests choose between answering a question about themselves (truth) or completing a chosen, and sometimes silly, activity (dare). Remember: Take turns so everyone gets to ask and answer, and don't dare someone to do anything that might make them hurt themselves.
8. **Groovy Girls makeovers!**
9. Play some fun party games (see pages 14 and 15).
10. **PILLOW FIGHT!**

Make a Sleepover **SLAMBOOK!**

What's a fun way to find out more about your friends?

Create a sleepover slambook in the pages of a super-personalized question and answer book. Not ready to tell all about your crush? No worries! You only have to reveal what feels right to you. Here are some examples:

When have you been the most scared?

What was the best present you've ever received?

What do you like best about yourself?

Rock Around the Clock

Music sets the mood. Whether you turn the dial to your favorite radio station, make your own mix, or buy a party theme CD—music is key. To get your PJ party rockin', hoppin', and boppin', check out these party tunes:

Feelin' Groovy
Simon and Garfunkel

It's My Party *Lesley Gore*

Girls Just Wanna Have Fun
Cyndi Lauper

Waitin' for Tonight *Jennifer Lopez*

Stop! In the Name of Love
The Supremes

Love Shack *The B-52s*

Rock Around the Clock
Bill Haley and His Comets

Who Let the Dogs Out
The Baha Men

Stayin' Alive
The Bee Gees

Happy Together
The Turtles

Gettin' Jiggy Wit It
Will Smith

The Twist
Chubby Checker

YMCA
The Village People

Summer Nights
Grease soundtrack

Walk Like an Egyptian
The Bangles

Terrific Treats to Eat

Reese's Recipe
Honey-Smeared Toast with Banana Smooshed on Top *(Serves 4)*

Ingredients:

4 slices of your fave bread

1 teaspoon honey per slice

2 bananas, peeled and sliced

Optional: 1 teaspoon butter per slice

Utensils: Toaster, plates, butter knife, small spoon

What You Do:

1. Toast all 4 slices until they're light brown, and place them on a plate.

2. Spread butter (if you like), then honey on the toast.

3. Arrange banana slices on top of the toast, and smoosh them into place with the back of a spoon.

Yvette's Very Delicious
Marshmallow Munchies *(Makes about 24)*

Ingredients:

3 tablespoons butter

1 10-ounce package (about 40) regular marshmallows, or 4 cups mini-marshmallows

½ teaspoon vanilla extract

6 cups puffed rice cereal

Cooking spray

Utensils: Large saucepan, spoon, measuring cups and spoons, spatula or waxed paper, 13 x 9 x 2-inch pan (or two 8 x 8 x 2 pans)

What You Do:

1. Ask an adult to melt the butter in a saucepan over low heat. Then add the marshmallows and vanilla. Stir until melted. Remove from the heat.

2. Add the puffed rice cereal into the saucepan, and stir until well-coated.

3. Using a buttered spatula or waxed paper, press the mixture evenly into a 13 x 9 x 2-inch pan coated with cooking spray.

4. Cut into 2-inch squares when cool. Enjoy!

Sweet Tart Friendship Frames

Showcase your friends in frames that are oh-so sweet...but not to eat!

What You Need: *(for one frame)*

- Polaroid camera (or a regular camera)
- Posterboard or cardboard cut into a 4¹/₂ x 4¹/₂-inch square in any color
- Four 4¹/₂-inch popsicle sticks
- Clear or white craft glue
- 1 roll of Sweet Tarts
- 8-inch-long piece of ribbon
- Tape

What You Do:

1. During your party, take photos of your guests. (If you don't have access to a Polaroid camera, use a regular camera, and send photos later to each friend.)

2. Lay out a cardboard square in front of you.

3. Decide which side will be the front of your frame. Put two sticks on opposite ends of the front side (they should be lined up right at the edges). Glue and press them in place. Repeat with the other two sticks to make a square and complete the frame.

(These two sticks will overlap the other two at the edges.) Let dry.

4. Take your Sweet Tarts candy and plan out a color pattern.

5. Glue your candy pattern to all four sticks. Let dry. Any candy that is left over is munchie material!

6. Slip your photo into the center of the frame and glue or tape it in place. (Trim photo to fit.)

7. Take the piece of ribbon, make a loop, and tape both ends together to the back of your frame, in the center. Let dry overnight.

13

Bring It On!

Wiggle Worms

Wiggles will turn into giggles when you play this sleeping bag relay race!

What You Need:
- Two sleeping bags
- A bag of gummy worms or licorice strings

What You Do:
1. Divide your guests into two teams.
2. When you shout "Go!", the first "worm" on each team jumps into the sleeping bag and wiggles on her belly to the finish line, where she grabs a gummy worm, gets up, runs back with the sleeping bag, and passes it to the next player on her team. Then, that teammate goes.
3. The first team to collect all its gummy worms and return to the starting spot wins!

Fashion Forward

Looking fashionable is a snap, right? Not when you add an element of surprise to the wardrobe department! Grab your gals together for this laugh-out-loud fashion game.

What You Need:
- An assortment of clothes (like tops, bottoms, belts, scarves, and hats. Make sure you have various colors and styles.)
- Paper and pens (1 for each friend)
- A watch

Musical Sleeping Bags

Here's a twist on musical chairs that's sure to have your friends racing for cover!

What You Need:

- One sleeping bag for each guest
- Your favorite music, and a boom box or stereo to play it on

What You Do:

1. Set down one sleeping bag for each player, except one. If you have six players, set out five sleeping bags. One player sits out the game to control the music.

2. Arrange the sleeping bags in a circle with the openings facing inward. Then, have the players stand at the closed end of the sleeping bags.

3. When you start the music, the players should walk in a circle around the sleeping bags. When the music stops, each player should quickly try to find a sleeping bag and get inside it. The player left without a sleeping bag is out of the game.

4. A player and a sleeping bag are removed with each round of play, until the winning player lands in the last sleeping bag!

What You Do:

1. Place all the clothes in one big pile, and hand out a pen and paper to each guest.

2. Time each guest as she hunts through the pile of clothes to design a groovy outfit. Give her one minute to put a *pizzaz-zy* outfit together.

3. When the time is up, all the other guests should judge her creation from 1 to 10 (10 is best) and write that number down next to her name on their piece of paper. Everyone should keep their scores secret until the end.

4. Continue to take turns until everyone has been the fashion designer. THEN, whichever pal is the best at math should tally up the scores. The outfit with the highest total score wins!

THE GROOVY GIRLS WERE HAVING A SLEEPOVER WHEN...

KNOCK KNOCK KNOCK

THERE WAS A LARGE PACKAGE WAITING FOR THEM.

To: The Groovy Girls

WHAT COULD BE INSIDE?

I THINK IT'S A WAVE RIDER!

I HOPE IT'S A HORSE!

I BET IT'S A DRUM SET!

WHAT DO YOU THINK IS INSIDE THE PACKAGE?

GO TO GROOVYGIRLS.COM TO FIND THE ANSWER.

groovygirls.com

Groovy Girls ®